THE SHADOW STEALER

Adapted by Jane B. Mason
Based on the television script by Ernie Jon
Illustrated by Aristides Ruiz

SCHOLASTIC INC.

New York Toronto London Auckland Sydney

ISBN 0-590-50205-0

Copyright © 1996 New Line Productions, Inc. All rights reserved.
THE MASK™ and related characters are trademarks of
New Line Productions, Inc.
Published by Scholastic Inc.

12 11 10 9 8 7 6 5 4 3 2 1   6 7 8 9/9 0 1/0

Printed in the U.S.A.   24

First Scholastic printing, January 1996

Stanley Ipkiss couldn't believe what he was reading. People were having their *shadows* stolen? How could that possibly be?

"Experts at Edge City's Criminal Investigations Bureau are stumped," Stanley read, "but many believe it to be the work of . . ." Stanley stopped reading and looked up. ". . . The Sinister Shadow Snatchers of Saturn?" he continued, shaking his head. He'd have to tell his reporter friend Peggy to stop getting her story ideas from bad movies.

Just then Stanley's friend Charlie came into the bank where they both worked — without his shadow!

Stanley's jaw dropped. "Charlie!" he exclaimed. "Your shadow . . . it's . . . "

"Gone. Yeah, I know," Charlie said. "I got cocooned by a black blob."

The shadow-stealer had struck again!

Later that night, Stanley took his dog, Milo, out for a walk. On the way home, Stanley got the spooky feeling he was being followed.

A second later Stanley was attacked by a black blob!

"Augh!" Stanley shrieked as the blob covered him from head to toe. "Get it off me!"

But the blob was already sucking up Stanley's shadow. And a minute later Stanley lay on the pavement — cold, pale, and shadowless.

A little while later, Stanley burst through his apartment door. "Saturn my foot!" he shouted. "A *shadow's* stealing shadows. But not for long," he said as he reached into his closet. It was time for . . . *The Mask!*

Stanley had found what looked like a plain, green, wooden mask floating in the river. But the mask had special powers. Whenever Stanley put it on, he became The Mask — a zany superhero with a weird green face. The Mask could do anything!

Stanley put the mask up to his face.

A bolt of lightning flashed. A tornado whipped around the room. When it finally stopped . . . The Mask appeared!

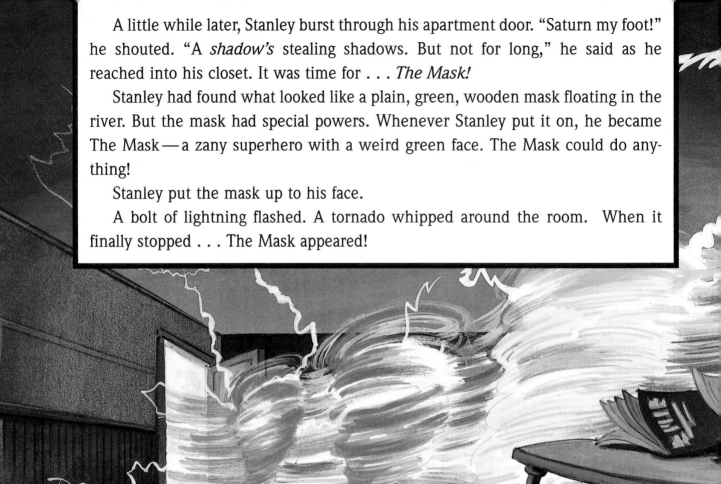

The Mask was ready for action. With a gust of wind, he disappeared out Stanley's door.

"Sssmokin'. . . " he said as he zipped down the hall and into the street. Suddenly, The Mask noticed his suspenders felt awfully tight. They were clenched in Milo's teeth!

Ka-zing! The Mask was yanked back into Stanley's apartment — and flattened against the wall. Lucky for him, he was a superhero. Being squished like a pancake didn't bother him a bit!

The Mask straightened himself out and dumped a huge pile of kibble into Milo's bowl. Then, quick as a wink, he disappeared again.

"Something is haunting the streets of Edge City," said The Mask as he strolled down a dark street. "Something wicked. Something weird."

The Mask had turned into a TV tabloid news host! "On tonight's episode of *Really Weird Bizarre Way-Out Funky Unbelievable and Unsolvable Mysterious Happenings,*" he said into a microphone, "we tackle the important questions about the shadow-stealing phenomenon."

He held up a finger. "One: *who* is behind it?"

He held up a second finger. "Two: *what* do they want?"

The Mask held up a third and final finger. "Three: *will* they give mine back?"

The Mask prowled the dark streets of the city, searching for the evil shadow-stealer.

He saw a woman about to be attacked by the shadow-thing. "Beware, Miss!" he cried. The woman saw The Mask, but she didn't see the black blob. "The Mask!" she screamed, turning to run away.

The Mask was confused. "Not the expected response . . . but *yes*, run like the wind and don't look back!"

But while The Mask watched the woman run down the street, he was engulfed in blackness. The shadow-thing!

"I'm blind!" The Mask cried. But the shadow-thing just stuffed The Mask into a shadow sack!

"C'mon," The Mask whined. "Lemme out of here!"

But the shadow-thing wasn't listening. Instead, it hefted the sack onto its back and flew straight up into the air!

Soon they arrived at an abandoned playground. The shadow-thing dumped The Mask onto the ground.

"A-ha!" The Mask said. "You *did* take me somewhere." He looked at the rusted old swing set. "And creepy, too," he added with a shudder.

Then he noticed something else — a spooky-looking kid was floating in front of him! The kid stretched his toe to the ground, and the shadow-thing became the kid's shadow!

The kid rushed up to The Mask. "Mask ol' buddy!" he said. "It's me, Skillit. I've been looking all over for you!"

The Mask shoved the kid away. "Get off! You're wrinkling my suit!" he shouted. Then he cleared his throat. "*Now* . . . I would appreciate your returning my shadow."

Skillit looked apologetic. "I never meant to take *your* shadow," he said.

Skillit lifted his own shadow off the ground, stuck his arm inside, and rummaged around. "Here it is," he finally said.

Once he had his shadow back, The Mask was ready to make tracks. But Skillit wanted to have some fun.

"I've got to be back in the Shadowland before the evening's up," he explained. "So let's go stir up trouble! It'll be just like old times!"

The Mask gave Skillit a you-must-be-crazy look. "I don't wanna hang around no creepy-face floating-in-midair shadow-snatching *kid*!" he told Skillit, strutting away.

Later that night, Stanley found out what The Mask had been up to.

"You get *all* the way to Mr. Shadow Snatcher and forget to bring everyone else's shadow back?!" Stanley scolded the wooden mask.

When he saw Milo, he became even angrier. The dog's stomach was huge! "And you overfed Milo!" he shouted.

Suddenly, a wave of evil laughter rolled through the room. Stanley saw a small boy with pointed ears and fangs step through his mirror!

Milo tried to lunge at the intruder. But his stomach was so big he could barely move!

Fzzzztt! Skillit used his finger to zap Milo with a bolt of green current!

"I've known *everyone* who's possessed the mask," Skillit said. "And you're not like Attila, Blackbeard, or Genghis. *They* were fun guys."

"They were monsters who caused suffering and terror!" Stanley cried.

But Skillit didn't answer. Instead, he scooped Stanley off his feet and pulled him out the open window!

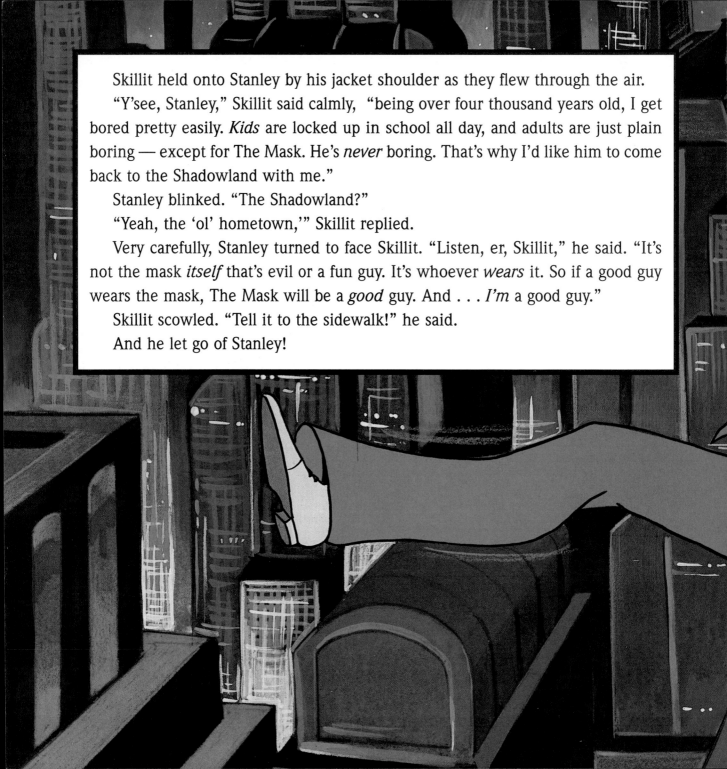

Skillit held onto Stanley by his jacket shoulder as they flew through the air.

"Y'see, Stanley," Skillit said calmly, "being over four thousand years old, I get bored pretty easily. *Kids* are locked up in school all day, and adults are just plain boring — except for The Mask. He's *never* boring. That's why I'd like him to come back to the Shadowland with me."

Stanley blinked. "The Shadowland?"

"Yeah, the 'ol' hometown,'" Skillit replied.

Very carefully, Stanley turned to face Skillit. "Listen, er, Skillit," he said. "It's not the mask *itself* that's evil or a fun guy. It's whoever *wears* it. So if a good guy wears the mask, The Mask will be a *good* guy. And . . . *I'm* a good guy."

Skillit scowled. "Tell it to the sidewalk!" he said.

And he let go of Stanley!

"Ahhhh!" Stanley screamed, as he plummeted toward the ground.

But Skillit was so busy thinking that he didn't notice what was happening to Stanley. "I may not be able to convince that Goody Two-shoes," Skillit said to himself. "But I *know* I can get The Mask to come to Shadowland with me."

"Heelllppp!" Stanley screamed again.

With half a second to spare, Skillit swooped down and scooped Stanley up. Then he hung him — by his jacket — on a flagpole!

"Okay, just keep the mask," Skillit told Stanley. "You do your thing with it, and when you're done with it, I'll talk to the next guy. Does that sound fair?"

Stanley nodded so hard his head hurt. "That sounds great!" he said.

Skillit grinned. "Good. After all, I'll live forever, and you won't."

"Uhh . . . one thing," Stanley called. "How *do* you stay eternal?"

"Why . . . I steal shadows, silly boy!" Skillit laughed an evil little laugh.

Stanley was horrified. "But that must mean you steal *their* youth!"

Skillit grinned again. "Oh sha-dowwww," he sang. His shadow appeared next to him, and Skillit pointed to a person on the street below. "*Sic 'em!*"

Stanley looked down and gasped. Skillit was pointing at his friend Peggy!

"Peggyyyy! Loooook out!" he shouted.

But he was too late. The shadow had already tackled her. A few seconds later, Peggy lay on the sidewalk, shivering.

Skillit flew away, leaving Stanley hanging on the flagpole!

As soon as Stanley had his feet back on solid ground, he went to Charlie's apartment.

But when he knocked, there was no answer.

Stanley took a few steps backward and — *CRASH!* — broke down the door. But he landed on top of the door in a belly flop. And when he looked up, Charlie was walking toward him. Well, sort of walking. Because Charlie was so old he could barely walk!

When Stanley saw Charlie, he knew the people of Edge City were in big trouble. And only one person could save the day . . . *The Mask!*

When Stanley got back to his apartment, he discovered that Milo had had his shadow stolen, too! He had turned into an old Milo!

"It's going to be okay," Stanley said, hugging old Milo. It had to be! Stanley grabbed the mask and slapped the lifeless wood onto his face.

Green lightning flashed. *KA-POW!* Stanley was The Mask.

"There are certain things in this world which are taboo!" he said grandly. "And messing with innocent dogs and baby seals is top of the list!" He tore out the door, a feeble old Milo following him.

Meanwhile, Skillit was at the abandoned playground. He knew The Mask would come to get the stolen shadows. Then Skillit could talk him into going to the Shadowland!

All of a sudden, a voice echoed through the night. "You're up wayyy past your bedtime, junior." It was The Mask!

"Hand over the shadows," The Mask ordered.

"Nooo!" Skillit howled. "You're not taking my youth!" He zoomed into the air — and dive-bombed straight toward The Mask!

The Mask zipped around, trying to convince Skillit to give the shadows back.
"Tch. Tch. Tch. Don't you know dive-bombing is impolite?" The Mask said.
Then The Mask whipped out a giant paddle.
"I think it's time someone met my friend *Mr. Manners*!"

"That's my boy!" he said, flattening Skillit's shadow.

Then The Mask turned into Kid Mask. "I'll give you a lick of my sucker *and* my one-of-a-kind Rosey O'Greer rookie card *if* you hand over the shadows," Kid Mask said.

But Skillit wouldn't give up his shadows. Instead, his shadow engulfed The Mask in a black blob!

The Mask was ready, though. He cut a hole in the shadow's stomach and climbed right back out — dressed as a Ninja!

But before he could move, a loud chime echoed through the air. Then something *really* weird happened: a swirling doorway appeared, right in the middle of the playground!

"What is *that*?" The Mask asked.

"The Shadowland," Skillit said. "I must enter before the thirteenth chime." He checked his watch. "That was number two."

The Mask looked at the doorway. "You wanted me to go in *there*?" he asked Skillit. "You're weirder than I thought."

Another chime sounded.

"If you come with me," Skillit said, "you could be The Mask forever, because Stanley Ipkiss would completely *cease* to exist!"

The Mask turned to Skillit with a grin. "Well, why didn't you *say* I could get rid of that drippy-dork neo-knob gip-noid Ipkiss in the first place?! You BET I'll go. *If* you hand over the shadows."

Skillit used his zapping finger to cut a hole right through the shadow's middle. All kinds of shadows spilled out, including Milo's.

Skillit pointed toward the doorway. "After you," he told The Mask.

But before The Mask stepped forward, he scooped up Milo into his arms. "Listen, Milo," The Mask said softly. "Daddy Mask has to go away for a little while."

Skillit tapped his foot impatiently. "We're kinda on a *schedule* here."

"I know, I know!" The Mask replied. He turned back to Milo. "Just one more thing," The Mask said. He leaned up close to Milo's ear and whispered so Skillit couldn't hear.

Finally, The Mask and Skillit stepped into the Shadowland doorway together.

But they didn't make it all the way to the Shadowland. Milo had The Mask's suspenders clenched in his teeth!

Ka-zing! The Mask and Skillit were yanked back through the doorway.

The Mask grabbed Skillit's shadow and wrung it out like a sponge. Lots more shadows spilled out!

Just then the twelfth chime sounded. "I must return!" Skillit said in a panic. But Skillit wasn't going anywhere. Milo had his shirt in his teeth!

Skillit's shadow tried to stay in Edge City, too. But he was pulled through the swirling Shadowland door. And a second later, Skillit was just a normal — well, a pretty funny-looking — kid.

"You don't understand," Skillit whined. "Without my shadow I'll grow *old*."

"In good time, Cubby," The Mask said. He had turned into a truant officer! "But first we have to get *you* to *school*. There's so much to look forward to . . . your first report card, your first bake sale. And all the kids in your class are gonna *looove* the new blue-face pointy-ear kid with the crazy shadowless look!"